D1287586

caillou®
favorite T-Shirt

Adaptation from the animated series: Jeanne Verhoye-Millet
Illustrations: CINAR Animation

"Catch the car, Teddy!"
Caillou has made up a new game.
He's rolling his toy cars down a ramp
made out of a long board.
Rosie walks into the room pulling her
toy ducky on a string.
"Can I play?" she asks.

"Okay," says Caillou. He turns to his little sister, and sees that she is wearing a T-shirt with teddy bears on it.

"No!" shouts Caillou. "That's my T-shirt! Take it off. It's mine!" He is very upset.

Mommy comes when she hears Caillou shouting. She tries to explain why Rosie is wearing Caillou's favorite T-shirt.

"Caillou, that T-shirt is too small for you, so I gave it to Rosie."

Caillou is so angry he is not listening to Mommy.

"It's not Rosie's! It's mine!" says Caillou with tears in his eyes.

"Okay, okay," says Mommy. "Rosie, let's go put on a different T-shirt."

Caillou pulls on his teddy bear T-shirt,
but it's not easy. He has to wriggle
and squirm like a caterpillar.
"Hmm... Aargh... Ow!" he says as
his ears get stuck in the neck of the
shirt.
Finally, Caillou says happily, "See?
It's not too small!" He marches
around the room with his bare tummy
showing.

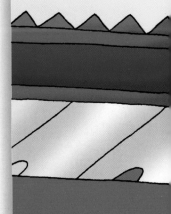

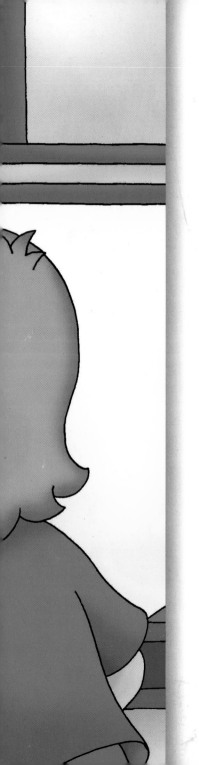

Rosie thinks Caillou looks very funny.
Maybe he's playing a new game.
She runs up to her brother and tickles
his tummy. "Coochy-coo!" she says,
giggling.
"Stop that," says Caillou. He knows
that the T-shirt used to cover his tummy
when he wore it.

Caillou stretches out to play with his cars, but his back gets cold and the carpet makes him feel itchy.

Caillou goes to his room. He doesn't want to play with his cars any more. He is too sad to do anything but sit with Teddy. Why did the T-shirt have to get too small?

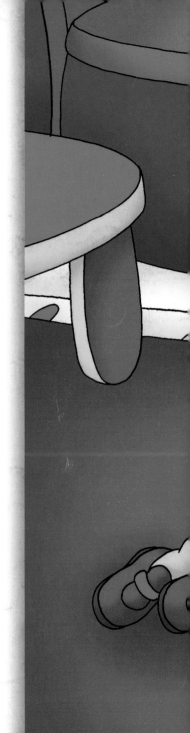

Mommy comes in and sits down beside Caillou. She has a photo album that she opens.

"Here's a picture of you on your second birthday," she says. "You look so cute and happy in your teddy bear T-shirt."

Caillou looks at the picture. He nods and says, "That's when I was little. I had my teddy shirt."

Mommy understands why Caillou
feels sad.
"Caillou, I'm sorry I gave your T-shirt
to Rosie," she says. "I forgot how
much you loved it. But now it's yours
again. Even if you don't wear it, you
can keep it as long as you want."

Caillou still loves his T-shirt. It's so
soft and cosy! But he knows he has
grown too big to wear it.
Caillou looks down at Teddy.
Suddenly, he knows what to do.
"I'm going to give it to Teddy,"
he says with a happy smile.
"Good idea, Caillou!" says Mommy.
She smiles too, as Caillou takes off
his favorite T-shirt and puts it on his
teddy bear.

Rosie comes into Caillou's room to
find Mommy. Look who's wearing the
T-shirt!
"Teddy's happy!" she giggles.
"Me too," says Caillou. He laughs
and hugs Teddy in his teddy bear
T-shirt.

© CHOUETTE PUBLISHING (1987) INC. and CINAR CORPORATION
All rights reserved. The translation or reproduction of any excerpt of this book in any manner whatsoever, either electronically or mechanically and, more specifically, by photocopy and/or microfilm, is forbidden.

CAILLOU is a registered trademark of Chouette Publishing (1987) Inc.

Text adapted by Jeanne Verhoye-Millet from the scenario of the CAILLOU animated film series produced by CINAR Corporation (© 1997 Caillou Productions Inc., a subsidiary of CINAR Corporation). All rights reserved.
Original story written by Christel Kleitch.
Illustrations taken from the television series CAILLOU.
Graphic design: Marcel Depratto
Computer graphics: CINAR Animation

Canadian Cataloguing in Publication Data

Verhoye-Millet, Jeanne
Caillou - Favorite T-shirt
(Scooter)
Translation of: Caillou: Le tee-shirt préféré
For children aged 3 and up.
Co-published by: CINAR Corporation.

ISBN 2-89450-283-4

1. Children's clothing — Juvenile literature. 2. Brothers and sisters —
Juvenile literature. I. CINAR Corporation. II. Title. III. Series: Scooter
(Montreal, Quebec).

TX340.V4713 2002   j391.3   C2001-941494-3

Legal deposit: 2002

We gratefully acknowledge the financial support of BPIDP, SODEC, and the Canada Council for the Arts for our publishing activities.

Printed in Canada
10 9 8 7 6 5 4 3 2 1